Kevin The Dodo

in

Fire and Ice

by **Alan Dickson**
and **Andy Statham**

Illustrations by Alan Dickson and Maani Khan

This is where our adventure takes us.

Ronnie marvelled at the view, "Hey guys just look at that!
The opera house looks really cool, a great shape for a hat."

Lucy smiled, "Oh Ronnie, I just love your mad idea."
Then she started waving, "Look my Auntie Quokka's here!"

Auntie Quokka hugged them all, as happy as could be.
"You're gonna love ole Sydney mates, there's such a lot to see.

I live in the mountains and the life there is the best,
Air is clear, the views are great, it's time to head out west."

They climbed into Aunt Quokka's truck, with Ronnie in the back.
It wasn't long before they reached her house along a track.

The house was small and cosy, just a cabin in the trees,
With flowers in the garden and the sound of buzzing bees.

Inside the cabin Auntie Quokka served them tea and cake.
"Miss Tara made all this for us, she really loves to bake.

And this is Tara, my best friend, a very friendly mouse.
She came to stay with me last year when fire burnt down her house."

"A lot of people lost their homes, the fires were bad last year."
Said Tara, as she looked around and wiped away a tear.

"This cake is great," said Ronnie, as he took a second bite.
"There's plenty more," said Tara, much to everyone's delight.

After tea they went outside to catch the evening breeze,
The sky glowed red and yellow as the wind blew through the trees.

But Ronnie looked unsettled as he sniffed the evening air,
"Can I smell something burning, are those flames that I see there?"

"Oh, no, you're right," Aunt Quokka gasped, "this could be a disaster.
The flames are getting very close, the fire is moving faster."

They all stared at the leaping flames and felt a sense of fear.
Aunt Quokka yelled, "It isn't safe, it's time we all left here!"

They ran towards Aunt Quokka's truck as thick smoke filled the air.
Aunt Quokka checked but realised that Tara wasn't there.

Then Ronnie said, "I'll go back in, I know I'll be alright."
With that he ran inside the house and disappeared from sight.

A burning branch exploded sending sparks into the sky,
They landed on the cabin roof, which now was tinder dry.

"Oh, Ronnie, do be careful!" Lucy screamed out to her friend.
The house was soon engulfed in flames ... could this be Ronnie's end?

The minutes passed, the friends were scared, then Ronnie reappeared,
But Tara wasn't with him, it was just as they had feared.

Aunt Quokka was in floods of tears, "Those fires they're a curse.
I know they happen every year but now they're getting worse."

"Why do you think they're getting worse?" asked Kevin, most concerned.
Aunt Quokka took a great big breath and told him what she learned.

"I've heard it said that climate change could be the cause of droughts.
Others say it's natural, of that I have my doubts.

The droughts are so much longer and they never seem to end,
Then lightning strikes and fires start and now I've lost my friend!"

They drove back down to Sydney so Aunt Quokka could recover
She stayed with friends, the rest went off to see what they'd discover.

They walked around the Sydney docks, and no one spoke a word.
Then Lucy whispered, "I'm so sad," she knew the others heard.

"We're all sad, Lucy," Ronnie said and Kevin nodded too,
"We need to occupy our minds and find some things to do."

Then Ronnie galloped off ahead in search of something new,
And came across a big red ship with penguins for a crew.

The other friends arrived in time to hear the penguins say,
"Please come aboard and look around, today's our open day."

"Hello," said Captain Polar, as he welcomed them aboard.
"Please stay a while, we'll tell you of the lands that we've explored."

Ravinder Singh, the penguin Mate, then pointed to the crew.
I'll let them introduce themselves and tell you what they do.

"I'm scientific officer, my name's Rosita Hinde,
I study changing climate and report on what I find.

"Is that like global warming?" Kevin asked, then she replied,
"Well, that comes first, then climates change, it cannot be denied."

Ravinder said, "We're heading south, we've room enough for you.
So come with us and you will see what climate change can do."

The ship set sail for southern seas, the crew sat down to dine.
The captain said, "You've heard some tales and now I'll tell you mine.

I once worked in a circus which is where I got this patch,
I wrestled giant crocodiles, I thought I'd met my match.

One mighty beast stood on my chest and pinned me to the floor…"
The crew began to giggle as they'd heard it all before.

Ravinder whispered to the friends, "We always hear this stuff.
His eye is fine, he wears the patch to make himself look tough."

The friends were with Rosita who explained what's going wrong,
"The world is in great danger and we haven't got too long.

Within a hundred years the earth could warm by three degrees."
"Isn't warm much better?" Ronnie laughed, "I hate to freeze."

"Oh, no," Rosita told him, "you will find that isn't true.
Just listen very carefully while I explain to you.

Crops are very sensitive to temperature and rain.
When they change, the food won't grow, and soon there'll be no grain.

I have a list of little things that we should do each day.
If everyone would try, we'd help this problem go away."

"Approaching the Antarctic!" Captain Polar called the crew.
"Everyone should come on deck, you won't believe the view.

Just watch the ice, it's breaking off and crashing to the sea,
A mighty smash, enormous splash, a chilling sight to see.

Looking through his telescope the captain gave a cry,
"I see a hut up on the ice, I can't believe my eye!

Those wisps of smoke mean someone's there, whoever could it be?
My books say no one's been up there since 1843."

"We really ought to help them," Lucy shouted, "we can't wait.
That ice could fall at any time, I hope we're not too late."

The captain ordered, "Take the boats, we'll head off to the shore!
Get your hats, your scarves and boots, you'll need them, that's for sure!"

They landed on the frozen shore and headed for the shack,
The ice around them creaked and groaned, they worried it might crack.

An hour passed and then at last Ravinder gave a cheer,
"A wooden hut there, dead ahead, but what's it doing here?"

Outside the hut were piles of logs and fish left out to dry.
They knocked upon the door quite hard, but there was no reply.

Kevin gently pushed the door and said, "Let's go inside."
The others followed nervously, who knew what they would find.

Kevin called, "Hello, hello, is anybody there?"
Across the room beside the stove he saw a panda bear.

The panda turned and then he smiled, "Oh please sit down, my dears.
I haven't seen another soul for more than ninety years.

I'm Captain George, you must be cold, now would you like some toast?
In winter time, I have to say, it's what I like the most.

When steam trains were invented I found out they caused pollution
So I came to Antarctica in search of a solution.

I found that if pollution should continue in that way,
The temperature would rise and then the ice would melt away.

I built this hut so far inland in 1843,
And now the ice shelf's melted I am right next to the sea."

With mugs of tea and buttered toast George gave his wise advice,
On polar exploration and his research into ice.

"There's so much information that we really want to know,"
Said Lucy, disappointed, but she knew they had to go.

Lucy turned to George and said, "Now you should leave this place.
Your home will soon be in the sea and lost without a trace."

"Of course, I know," said Captain George, "and all good things must end,
But my home's here yet even so it's good to have a friend.

And you, big Ronnie, please take care, the ice is not so strong."
Ronnie reassured him that the journey wasn't long.

And as they left they turned and saw old George their friendly host,
Who seemed to walk straight through the wall in search of extra toast.

"He was nice," said Lucy, "But I hope his hut won't fall."
"Nice, but strange," said Ronnie, "he just walked right through a wall!"

But as they spoke they heard a crack, the ice had melted through.
Poor Ronnie slipped, he slid, he fell then disappeared from view.

Ravinder and the crew looked shocked, "What are we all to do?"
"Don't Panic", Captain Polar said, "I haven't got a clue."

Then Kevin found a length of rope and made it quite secure.
"Don't go!" Yelled Captain Polar, "it's too dangerous for sure!"

But Kevin knew he couldn't wait and grabbed the other end.
"I'm on my way," he shouted to his pachydermal friend.

With that he jumped into the crack where Ronnie now was stuck.
"Don't worry, I will get you out of here with any luck!"

He tied the rope round Ronnie's waist, and told the crew to lift,
But Ronnie was no featherweight, so movement wasn't swift.

They pulled and heaved and then at last the rhino reappeared.
"Wow, that was fun," grinned Ronnie, Lucy whispered, "You're just weird."

The friends all laughed, but then Ravinder looked at them quite stern,
"It's getting late and so it's time that we should now return."

The captain smiled and looked confused, "I need to change my hat."
Ravinder and Rosita smiled, "He's always saying that."

Back on board the ship they went in search of information
About the friendly Captain George's lonely isolation.

Kevin said, "Now gather round, it's here on WikiWho.
That George went to Antarctica in 1842!

Even then he thought pollution might be causing harm,
But sadly disappearing without raising the alarm.

"We thought we saw him passing through the wall in search of toast."
Asked Lucy, "Do you think this means that we just saw a ghost?"

"Ghost or not," Rosita spoke, "The words he said were true.
Climate change is threatening the world that we once knew."

Captain George of the Antarctic

Captain George was an early eco-warrior and was one of the first to recognise the harm being done to the planet at the start of the Industrial Revolution.

Captain George thought that steam engines and factories that pumped out pollution would damage the atmosphere so in 1842 he started on a journey that saw him end up in Antarctica.

By 1843 Captain George had set up a base camp in Antarctica and early messages received from him said that he was already finding traces of pollution but unfortunately no-one really listened. Captain George was the first to warn the world about climate change and the dangers of melting ice at the Poles.

By the end of 1843 nothing more was ever heard from Captain George and it was presumed that he was lost forever.

Search Wikiwho

Home Page
All about everything
Famous things
Famous adventurers
Contact Us

Add to Wikiworld
Edit pages

WIKIWHO

Captain George

Captain George in 1840

Born   August 18 1800
Died   Unknown
Sea Captain and Explorer

They left the cold Antarctic, where their breath would quickly freeze,
To sail back to Australia across the stormy seas.

Embarking from the ship they bid the crew a fond farewell,
And there upon the quay they saw Aunt Quokka looking well.

To their surprise, right next to her was Tara, "She's alive!!"
Lucy called out to the mouse, "So how did you survive?"

"Well, when I saw you running round, I couldn't match your pace.
I jumped into Aunt Quokka's pouch, it seemed the safest place."

The friends all laughed and looked relieved, so happy all was well.
Then Kevin interrupted, "I don't mean to break the spell.

Remember that Rosita had a list of things to do,
That help to slow down climate change, it's really up to you.

Let's take some time and think about the way the world's transforming
And see what we can do ourselves to combat global warming."

What is climate change?

How climate change affects coral reefs

Climate Kids, NASA

Be an energy saver

What if the ice caps melted? (Video)

Hong Kong Museum of Climate Change

What is renewable energy?

What causes sea level rise? (Video)

The importance of trees. (Video)

What is climate change? (Video)

Climate change. What can I do?

Animals affected by climate change

Secret Message

Meet Kevin and his friends in their other adventures.

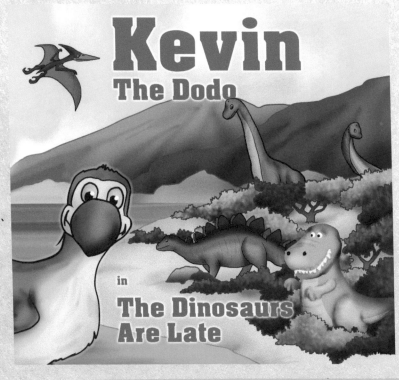

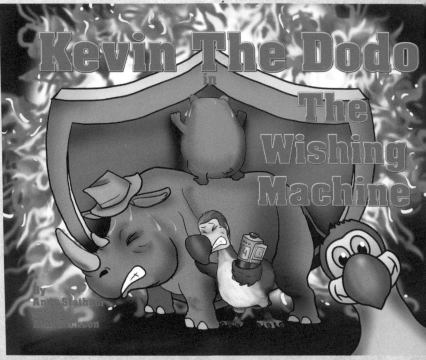

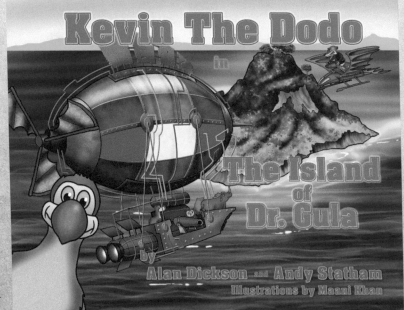

This book was produced in collaboration with the Jockey Club Museum of Climate Change in Hong Kong. The authors would like to thank Mr George SK Ma and his team at the museum for their invaluable assistance.

JOCKEY CLUB MUSEUM OF CLIMATE CHANGE

The Jockey Club Museum of Climate Change was established in December 2013 at The Chinese University of Hong Kong. It is the first museum of its kind in the world. Among its various activities, it regularly organises interactive multimedia exhibitions, featuring valuable collections and providing information about climate change. These exhibitions are designed to keep visitors abreast of the latest developments in environmental conservation and sustainability and to persuade them, especially students and teachers, to rally to the cause of environmental stewardship. Since its inception, the museum has hosted over 1.2 million exhibition visitors and served millions of members of the public through its off-site educational activities.

More details about the Museum can be found at https://www.mocc.cuhk.edu.hk/.

This book is dedicated to all the young adventurers out there, just like Kevin, Lucy and Ronnie, who care for the world they live in and want to make sure it survives for future generations to live in safely.

"Kevin The Dodo in: Fire and Ice" by Alan Dickson & Andy Statham
Published by Alan Dickson in Hong Kong
https://www.kevinthedodo.com
©2022 Alan Dickson & Andy Statham
ISBN: 978-988-74957-6-5

CPSIA information can be obtained
at www.ICGtesting.com
Printed in the USA
BVHW060906300922
648371BV00016B/4